SPACE PIRATE

By
Henry Bamman
William Odell
Robert Whitehead

Illustrations
Roger Herrington

BENEFIC PRESS

Westchester, Illinois

Space Science Fiction Series

Space   Pirate
Milky   Way
Bone   People
Planet   of   the   Whistlers
Inviso   Man
Ice   Men   of   Rime

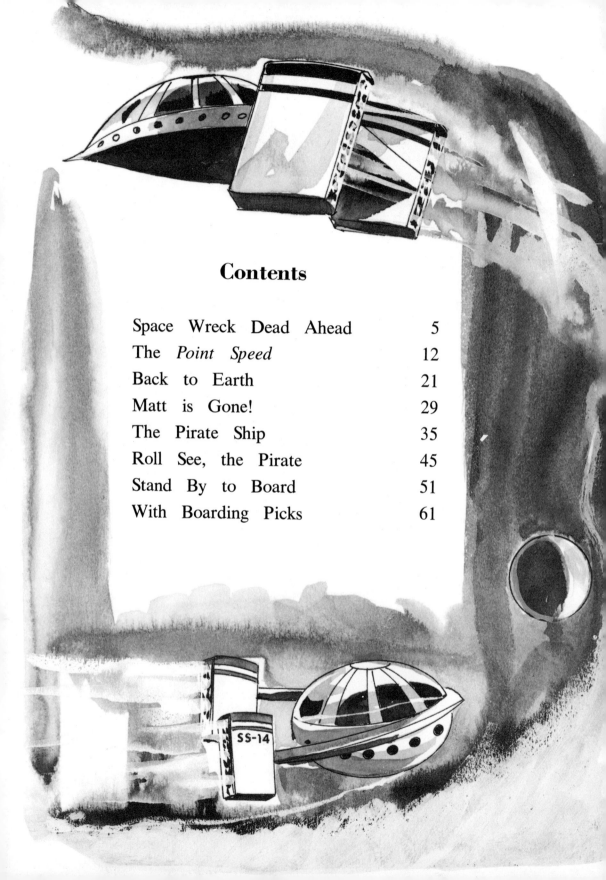

Contents

Space Wreck Dead Ahead!

Scotty Good did not have to see the rocketship speeding in on them through space. The lights going on and off on the spacefeeler board in front of him told Scotty the other ship was there. Jerry Black knew there was a rocketship out there, too.

"Watch it now, Scotty!" Jerry called out. "That rocketship is moving in on us. It's only 2,000 miles away— and closing in on us fast!"

Scotty rolled the big spacesweeper, the *SS-14*, to the right. But the spacefeeler board told him that the other ship had turned to its left. Now the two ships had closed to 1,000 miles. In no time they would be hitting head-on.

"What are those men in that rocketship doing?" Scotty asked. "They should be turning away. Have Matt give me two more engines, Jerry."

5

"Right away, Scotty!" Jerry said. He called into the inside-talker. "Matt, turn on two more engines—and hurry!"

A man's voice called back. "Engine 1-A firing! Engine 2-A firing!"

Scotty could feel the *SS-14* move ahead fast as the two engines cut in. Fire shot out the back end of the top rocket engine on the left side of the spaceship. Scotty turned in his seat to watch as the rocket fire ran off into black space behind the ship. Then he saw the lights from the other rocketship sweep by them.

"There goes the rocketship," Scotty said to Jerry. "I can see his lights. He is about 50 miles away."

"But at the speed these spaceships go, that was still too close," said Jerry. "I'm going to see the head of the Space Police about that ship when we get back to Earth."

The spacesweeper roared on into space. Scotty looked at his friend, Jerry Black, seated at his side in the spaceship. Jerry was top man on the *SS-14*. He knew more about space sweeping than any other man in the Space Police. Jerry, Scotty Good and the rocket engine man, Matt Miles, had been sent out to find the wrecked Space Police ship *Point Speed* and to bring it in.

Jerry was listening closely to the spacetalker on the space-feeler board in front of them. The spacetalker told the men if there were meteors or other rocketships close to them. Just then a voice from the spacetalker said, "There is a two-engined spaceship dead ahead. Bring the *SS-14* two points to the right."

Scotty moved the *SS-14* two points to the right as the spacetalker had told him to do. As Scotty turned the ship

back to the left again, Jerry turned to him and said, "We are getting close to the wrecked spaceship, Scotty. Will you call Matt on the inside-talker? I want to give him an engine speed."

Scotty put in a call to Matt. Matt Miles was the only other man on the spaceship. Matt was a little man, just right for working around inside a rocket engine.

"Engine room here," came Matt's voice over the inside-talker. "Go ahead."

"As I see it, Matt," said Jerry, "the wrecked rocketship *Point Speed* is about 14,000 miles dead ahead. It is right in a meteor belt between Point A-1 and Point B-2."

Matt Miles asked, "Are we going in there? With all of those meteors? How will we get out?"

Jerry was about to say something to Matt on the inside-talker when Scotty cut in. "We will be all right, Matt. Jerry knows what he is doing. If he says he can get the *SS-14* into the meteor belt, he can get it out, too."

"All right," said Matt. "Jerry is running the ship. But after we are hit by a meteor, we will be dead a long time."

"Listen, Matt," said Jerry over the inside-talker. "If you have seen a wrecked ship rolling in space, you know what we are here for. We are to sweep this dead ship out of space and pull it back to Earth. All of the men on that rocketship are long dead. The ship is just roaring up and down in space. If we don't get that ship out of there, it will run head-on into other ships."

"Jerry is right, Matt," said Scotty. "If we Earth Space Police don't come out here and pull our own wrecks back to Earth, what will spacemen from other planets do about their wrecks? I will tell you. Nothing!"

"Just think what that would do to our work in space," Jerry said. "And what if space pirates get to that wrecked ship? Pirates could use the rockets and that speed-shot they will find on board."

"Matt, you knew what it would be like when you got into the Space Police," Scotty said. "If we have to make a run through a meteor belt, we do it."

"All right, all right you two!" said Matt. "What speed do you want, Jerry?"

"Top speed! Ahead!" said Jerry.

"Meteor belt, here we come," Matt called out over the inside-talker.

9

Jerry watched the spacefeeler board very closely now. "Here comes the first meteor, men," he called out. "It's at Point A-1, and about 500 miles away." Into the inside-talker Jerry said, "Cut back on engine two, Matt. Give me all you have on engine one."

"Move the spaceship one point to the right, Scotty," Jerry called out again. "Now back to the left, Scotty. Watch out! There is another meteor dead ahead - run us more to the right, Scotty - to the right! Good! We are by that one. Give us engine two again, Matt. Look out, Scotty, here comes another one! Pull up, Pull up!"

The talk between Jerry, Scotty and Matt went on for some time as they made their run into the meteor belt. Scotty had just turned the head of the spaceship down when he saw a spacefeeler light come on over Jerry's head. From this light the men knew that *SS-14* was closing in very fast on something bigger than their own spaceship.

Jerry turned up the sound on the spacefeeler board. He and Scotty listened closely to the spacefeeler as it sent its sound out into space. The sound hit something in front of them, and came right back to the ship. Jerry could tell by the way the sound came back and hit the spacefeeler light above his head that they had come on a slow-moving spaceship.

"It's the wrecked rocketship, dead ahead!" Jerry called out.

"How do you know?" Matt asked.

"There is no sound from her," said Jerry. "All on board are dead. Her engines are stopped."

"She is just 100 miles away," said Scotty. "Right between A-1 and B-2."

"Just as I said it would be," Jerry called out. "Cut back on the engines, Matt. Keep the sweepers head up, Scotty. We are going in."

(1126)

11

The *Point Speed*

Scotty could see the wrecked spaceship with his own eyes now. She was a great dark thing against the greater darkness of space. The dead ship was coming up on their left side. The *SS-14* moved slowly toward the wrecked rocketship, coming closer and closer.

"Only 20 miles away," said Scotty. "This will be..."

Just then Jerry cut in. "A meteor! A meteor!" he called out. "Right behind the wreck! Cut engine one, Matt! Pull the ship to the left, Scotty!"

Scotty saw the meteor then. It had come out of space from behind the wrecked ship. The spacefeeler had not seen the meteor. It had sounded on the wreck. Now the meteor was headed right for them and moving very fast!

Scotty turned the front of the *SS-14* to the left. As he did, rocket engine one cut out. And just in time. The big meteor roared over the top of the *SS-14*, a little behind it. Scotty could see the meteor as it sped into space.

Just then Matt called out over the inside-talker. "Jerry! Scotty! The wrecked rocketship! We are right on top of it! The two ships are going to hit!"

"Pull up, Scotty!" Jerry called out.

Scotty had no time to pull up. All at once the *SS-14* rolled to the right. The roll pulled Scotty from his seat. His head hit something. Scotty had the feeling he was turning over and over in space. Then.....nothing!

Scotty opened his eyes. He could hear the voices of Jerry and Matt close by. Scotty moved to get up, but he could not make it. Jerry and Matt came over to help him.

"What happened?" Scotty asked. "I feel as if I have been belted by a hit-and-run spaceship."

"You hit your head when the ship rolled," said Jerry. "You have been out for some time."

"I thought we had run into that wrecked rocketship," said Scotty. "But if we had, we would not be talking. We would be dead. What happened?"

"We hit the *Point Speed*, all right," said Matt. "But just before we did, I turned on the magnets. With our magnets on, the two ships came together slowly. Right now the two ships are running side by side through space."

"Do you feel all right, Scotty?" Jerry asked. "Can we board the wreck now?"

"I'm all right," Scotty answered. "Let's go. There is a lot of work to do."

"We are through the meteor belt," said Jerry. "We can take our time now. But let's get with it."

Before boarding the ship the men took a closer look at the wreck of the *Point Speed* through the spaceteller. The spaceteller was a light that took pictures of meteors and other things in space. Then the spaceteller sent the pictures back to the *SS-14*.

Jerry turned on the spaceteller. He let the light sweep over the dead ship. *Point Speed* was a big rocketship. She was loaded from front to back with small spaceship engines, fire rockets and speed shot. The Space Police used the fire rockets and the speed shot to gun down space pirates. The load was still on board.

Point Speed had not come back to Earth from its run to the Black Planet. The Space Police thought that *Point Speed* had come on a big meteor belt. The meteors would have hit the sides of the spaceship and made holes, letting the air out. With the men on board dead, the ship would then roll through space—running into police rockets, hitting other spaceships, and cutting down spaceworkers on their way through space. The wrecked ship had to be pulled out of space and taken back to Earth.

"She is a big one," said Jerry as he looked at the pictures. "But we can move her. First, let's take a look inside."

The men got into their space suits. The space suits were very light, with small rockets in the belts. With the belt rockets and a small rocket gun, a man could move around very well outside a spaceship.

"Matt," said Jerry. "Cut a hole in the side of *Point Speed*. I can see what looks like meteor holes in her, but

they are too small for us to get through. Once we are inside the wreck, look around and see if the ship has some of its meteor gas left. If there is any, we can use it. We used more than I wanted to use when we came through the meteor belt."

"Jerry and I will go up front in the wreck," said Scotty. "We will put a magnet line on the ship. Then we can pull the ship behind us and back to Earth."

"All right, men," said Jerry. "Let's go!"

It did not take Matt very long to cut a hole into the side of *Point Speed*. The first cut was into the engine room. Once they were inside, the men could see that there was still a little of the meteor gas on board the wreck. They could use it on the *SS-14*. Matt was left behind to run a gas line from the engine room of the wrecked ship to the *SS-14*.

Jerry and Scotty worked their way to the top of the ship. Along the way they found two dead men. Up front in the ship they found the man who had run the ship. His head was back and his eyes open. His eyes were looking up at a hole in the top of the spaceship. Through that hole had come a fire rocket, not a meteor.

"Space pirates did this!" Scotty said.

"Let's move this man out of his seat," Jerry said. "I want to look at the spacefecler board. It could tell us more about what happened here."

Scotty walked back through the ship. The door to one room was open, and Scotty looked in. A dead man was there. He was on his side with his face down. Scotty pictured what had happened here. The man had heard air sweeping through the spaceship. He had opened the door.... and all the air was gone.

16

Scotty looked into another room. There were no other dead men in the room. As it was, there was nothing in the room. But there should have been. Scotty knew that this room on any Space Police ship was the rocket keep. In the keep there should have been long lines of police rockets and space guns. But all of them were gone now.

Scotty heard Jerry walk into the room. Scotty turned around. "They got all of the fire rockets, Jerry," Scotty said. "But who did it?"

Jerry handed Scotty a small paper. "This will tell you," said Jerry. "Take a look at this paper."

Jerry handed over the paper, and Scotty took a close look at it. The paper said:

> Roll See, the Pirate,
>   Has taken your rockets.
> Do you know how or when?
> And all your spacesweepers
>   And all your spacemen,
> Can't get the rockets back again.

"Roll See, the Space Pirate!" said Scotty. "That just can't be!"

"I know it!" said Jerry. "Roll See's pirate ship went down on the Fire Planet 10 years ago. No man has come back from the Fire Planet. Roll See is dead!"

"How could it be Roll See?" Matt asked. "We all know he is dead."

"We *think* he is dead," said Jerry.

"Could another space pirate be using his name?" asked Matt. "Pirate ships have been seen over Planet Tookk and Planet Way."

"Could be," said Scotty. "Still, it looks to me as if Roll See wrecked *Point Speed*. This is the way he worked."

"And talking of work, let's do more of it," said Jerry. "We want to get back to Earth before the day is over."

(1298)

Back to Earth

Jerry, Scotty and Matt were working over the wrecked spaceship. They were getting ready to pull the rocketship back to Earth. They were sealing all the rocket and meteor holes in the sides of the ship. In that way the ship would hold in the air the men were going to put into it.

"You say that Roll See wrecked ships in this way, Scotty," Matt said. "How did he work?"

"The first spaceship that Roll See pirated was hit about fifteen years back," Scotty said. "That was before you came into the Space Police, Matt. It was a worker's rocketship running between the Planet Tookk and the Planet Way. Roll See and his pirates gassed that ship. The workers were all dead when we got to them."

"Then Roll See shot down a Space Police rocketship," Jerry said. "He got away with all its fire rockets. Other spaceships were shot down, too. Roll See always left a paper with funny writing on it, like the paper I found on this spaceship."

"What happened to Roll See?" asked Matt.

"For a year Roll See got away with what he was doing," said Jerry. "But one day a big Space Police ship closed in on him over the Fire Planet. Roll See and his pirate friends made a run for it. But their spaceship must have run out of meteor gas. The pirate ship went down on the Fire Planet. The Space Police turned away just in time. No ship that has been pulled down into the Fire Planet has come out again!"

"And that was the end of Roll See?" asked Matt.

"That's what we thought," said Jerry.

"Well, I know something," said Scotty, looking around the room. "I have sealed another hole in the ship and that is all of them. Now we can get out of here."

Jerry turned to Matt. "Is the magnet line between *SS-14* and *Point Speed* on all right?" he asked.

"We are ready to go," said Matt.

"Good work," said Jerry. Turning to Scotty, he said, "Get back on board the *SS-14*. Run an air line in here. Then I want you to ready the ship's engines. It is time we were on our way back to Earth."

"If Scotty is going to run the engines, what will I do?" Matt asked.

"We used up a lot of our meteor gas coming through that meteor belt," Jerry said. "We have to go back through that belt now. Pulling *Point Speed* will take a lot of gas. If we are close to running out of gas, Scotty and I will cut the line between the ships. Then we will go on to Earth, gas up, and come back for you and the rocketship. We can fire the magnet line to you. That way we will not have to stop again."

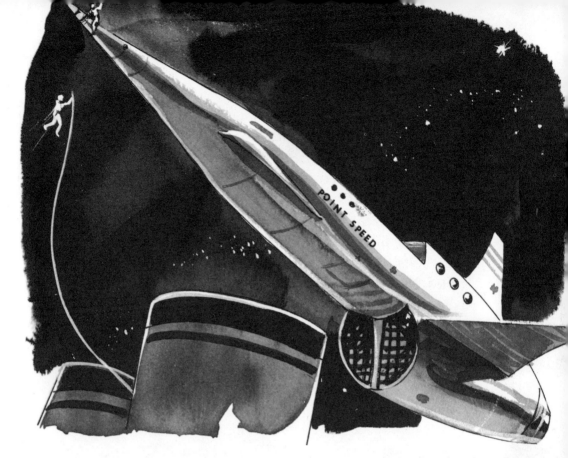

"How can you tell where to find me?" asked Matt.

"We will place you in the pull of Planet Tookk," said Scotty. "Once there you will just go around and around that planet."

Matt thought, then said, "All right, I will do it. But do just one thing for me before you go. Run air into this ship. If you don't, I will be dead in no time."

"We like you, Matt," said Scotty.

"We will do it—for a friend," Jerry said.

Scotty took his place at the firing board in the space-sweeper. At one time Scotty had been an engine man. His hands ran over the firing board, putting together the rocket engines that would move *SS-14* and the dead ship, *Point Speed*.

Jerry turned off the side magnets and *Point Speed* rolled slowly away from the spacesweeper. Jerry called for rocket engine one and the *SS-14* moved a little ahead of *Point Speed*. The wrecked ship was now at the end of the magnet line, being pulled by the spacesweeper *SS-14*.

Jerry got into his seat and belted himself down. Over the inside-talker he told Scotty and Matt to put on their seat belts. After that he said, "Be ready for a pull of 20 times that on the Planet Way, men. With *Point Speed* behind us, it is going to take a lot of pull to get us moving. Got that?"

"Got it!" Scotty and Matt called back.

Jerry listened for the engines. When they sounded just right to him, he said, "Ready in the engine room!"

Jerry ran his hand down along his seat belt. "Two!"

Jerry put his head back against the seat. "One!"

"Fire!"

The *SS-14* roared up and up at great speed. Its big rocket engines—made to move ships ten times bigger than *Point Speed*—pulled the wrecked rocketship after it. In no time the two ships—one behind the other—were roaring through space at 1,000 miles an hour.

"How did you like that take-off, Scotty?" Jerry called into the spacetalker.

"Great! Just great!" said Scotty.

"How are you feeling, Matt?" Jerry asked.

"I'm feeling all right now," said Matt. "I thought I had been shot from a gun."

"If you think that was something," said Jerry, "watch out! My spacefeeler board just came on. Here we go into that meteor belt again."

The *SS-14* roared into the meteor belt at 1,000 miles an hour. Jerry had his work cut out for him. Up and down through space went the spacesweeper, with *Point Speed* rolling along behind. In and out between the meteors went the two ships—turning right, then left, speeding up, then slowing down. Then all at once the two ships were through the meteor belt.

"We have made it, men!" Jerry called out over the space-talker. "We..."

Just then Scotty's voice cut in. "Jerry, rocket engine 1-S just ran out of gas! Top engine 1-A will run out before we go another 500 miles. We are not going to make it back to Earth with this wreck in back of us. We are using gas fast. We will have to cut away from *Point Speed*. Now is a good time. We are coming up on the Planet Way."

Matt's voice came on the spacetalker. "Do you think there are any other Space Police ships close by that could take me in?" he asked.

"No," said Jerry. "I thought about that before we took off. I called Earth, but they could not help. They said something about the men having a day off."

"I should have taken the day off, too," said Matt. "Well, go ahead. Cut the line. But—do come back for me, friends."

Jerry turned off the magnet line between the two ships. Then he rolled the *SS-14* to the right and away from the *Point Speed*.

"You have air for two days, Matt," said Jerry. "But we will have you back on Earth before this day is over."

"See you around, Matt," Scotty called out. "Put on your space suit when you go out for a walk."

"Fun-ny!" Matt called back.

Then the spacesweeper roared away into space at top speed. Jerry looked back. He could see *Point Speed* as it rolled behind the Planet Way. Jerry did not know it at the time, but when he saw his friend Matt again, Matt would be in the hand of Roll See, the pirate!

(1335)

Matt Is Gone!

The *SS-14* roared over the face of the earth, then slowed. Jerry turned the rocketship on end. Scotty cut back on the rocket engines.

Before the two men could get out of their seats, the spacetalker lights on the spacefeeler board went on. A man's voice said, "To the men in *SS-14*. Don't ·get out of your ship. We have work for you to do."

"We have work to do," Jerry called back. "We have to gas up and go back to the Planet Way. Matt Miles is still out there in the wrecked spacerocket *Point Speed.*"

"We know that," said the voice. "We heard you over the spacetalker. But we think a Space Police ship has gone down on Planet Tookk, and we want you to take a look."

"Scotty's voice cut in and asked, "Why do we have to go? Planet Tookk is out of our way. And we do have to pick up *Point Speed.*"

"We have no other ships ready," said the man. "And Tookk is only a little out of your way."

Jerry turned down the spacetalker. "The man is right, Scotty," he said. "Tookk is only about 75,000 miles away from Planet Way. We can go to Tookk, have a look-see, then stop by and pick up *Point Speed* and Matt on our way back."

"Well, I don't like it," said Scotty. "But there is nothing we can do about it."

Jerry turned back to the spacetalker and said, "We will take a look for that ship down on Tookk. But before we go, we have to have meteor gas and a rocket engine man."

"They are as good as there right now," said the man.

"By the way," Jerry asked over the spacetalker. "What do you know about a space pirate named Roll See?"

"We heard you using his name," said the man on the other end of the line. "We are getting together our papers on him now. When you get back, we can talk about him."

"Good," said Jerry. "We should not be gone too long. It is only 75,000 miles to Tookk, and another 30,000 to Planet Way."

Once again in space, Jerry was at the spacefeeler board, his eyes and hands running over it with great speed. Scotty was at his side. When the *SS-14* was about 5,000 miles away from Planet Tookk, the spacefeeler board picked up the sound of a spaceship moving in on them.

"I would like to know a lot more about Roll See," Scotty said. "From what I have heard he must have been quite a space pirate in his day."

The sound of the spaceship on the spacefeeler board came in stronger and the men forgot about the pirate.

30

"There is a small spaceship coming in on our left," Jerry called out into the inside spacetalker. "It is moving fast and coming right in on us. Cut back on engine one in the engine room. Slowly bring *SS-14* to the left one point, Scotty. Then the rocketship can get by us."

Scotty turned the big ship to the left. Jerry looked at the spacefeeler board. The lights on the board told him that the spaceship coming at them had turned a little to its right. The two ships were still headed for one another.

"What is going on here?" Jerry said. "That ship is trying to run us down!"

"Call him on the open spacetalker," said Scotty. All ships in space had to keep their open spacetalkers on at all times. In that way the men could hear calls from other spaceships when they needed help.

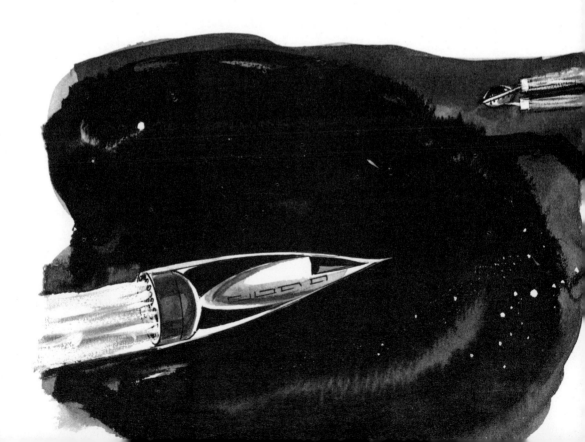

Before Jerry could say a thing, a man's voice said, "To the big spacesweeper headed for Tookk. Give way. We are going in front of you. That is all."

"That tops all!" said Jerry, looking at Scotty. Jerry turned back to the open spacetalker and said into it, "Listen! I don't know who you are. But this is the *SS-14*, a Space Police ship. All ships headed for planets have the right-of-way. You know by our heading we are going to Tookk. Now, get that rocketship out of the way!"

No call came back over the open spacetalker. But two of the lights of the spacefeeler board went out.

Scotty said, "We are coming into the pull of Planet Tookk, Jerry. Do you want to take a look from up here, or go in closer?"

"Let's cut right through," said Jerry. "If there is a ship down there, let's find it fast. We still have to pick up Matt."

"All engines ahead!" Scotty called.

Jerry took the spacesweeper in close to the planet, then slowly around it. Tookk was a small, dead planet, with only a light gas over it. From the spacesweeper one could see all of the planet. There was no Space Police ship or any other ship down on the planet.

"Where do you think Earth heard that there was a ship out here?" Scotty asked.

"I think a rocketship saw a light over this way," said Jerry. "The men on it thought a ship was on fire."

"Let's be on our way," said Scotty. "We have to pick up Matt."

"Right you are," said Jerry. "See if you can get him on the spacetalker. He could be listening in."

"*SS-14* to *Point Speed*," Scotty called. "Are you there, Matt? Come in."

SS-14

Scotty turned up the spacetalker. The two men listened. Matt did not call back.

Scotty called again. No sound came back to them over the spacetalker.

"That's funny," said Jerry. "I told him to keep his spacetalker open."

"What do you think, Jerry?" asked Scotty. "Is his spacetalker not working?"

"I think that's it," said Jerry.

"He could be out of air," Scotty said. "And..."

"Matt had more air than he could use," said Jerry. "He is all right. You will see."

Jerry called the engine room and had the engines run up to top speed. It was not long before the *SS-14* picked up *Point Speed* on the spacefeeler board. Jerry called the wrecked ship again. Matt did not call back.

"We will have to go in close and use the magnets," said Jerry. "With Matt's spacetalker not working, he can't hear us tell him how to put on the magnet lines."

Slowly, Jerry rolled the two ships together. Little by little *SS-14* moved in on *Point Speed*. Then—the two ships hit. Scotty and Jerry put on their space suits, took their hand rocket guns, and made their way through the door of *SS-14* and into the spaceship *Point Speed*.

"Matt, where are you?" Jerry called out.

But Matt did not call back.

Scotty and Jerry went through the wrecked ship from front to back. Matt was not to be found.

"He is just not here!" said Scotty.

"But how can he be gone?" asked Jerry. "There is no place to go to out here but into—into space."

(1167)

The Pirate Ship

Scotty heard the voice coming to them through *Point Speed's* inside-talker. The engine room man on the *SS-14* was calling.

"It's a small spaceship, Scotty," said the man. "I can just see it. It's headed right for us. I don't like her looks. It could be a pirate ship!"

"Jerry! Back to the *SS-14*!" Scotty called out. "There is another ship closing in on us!"

Jerry ran through *Point Speed*. Scotty was right behind him. Once they were back on board the *SS-14*, Jerry turned on the spacefeeler board. There was a ship closing in on them. It was a slow-moving ship, and it had turned to come up on the right side of the *SS-14*.

"It's small to be a pirate ship," said Jerry. "But still, let's man the fire rockets on your side, Scotty."

To the rocket engine man Jerry said, "Keep your eyes open back there. We don't know who is on the ship, or what they want. Could be they just want to help us. Then, again, it could be a pirate ship."

Scotty manned the fire rocket. The fire rocket was a big gun. It fired two small rockets at one time. One rocket could bring down a spaceship if the rocket hit in the right place. Jerry turned up the open spacetalker, then loaded a space gun. The space gun fired small shot about as big as a man's hand. A piece of shot had a small magnet in it. When fired, the shot headed right for the ship it was fired at. The ship pulled the magnet-loaded shot right to it.

All at once a voice came over the open spacetalker. "SS-14! We have you under our guns. You can't get away. Give up before we open fire!"

"I can see them now," called the man in the engine room. "But I don't see that they have any big guns. Our ship is bigger than theirs. Let me give it to them."

"Hold it!" Scotty called out. "Fire only when Jerry or I tell you to."

To the man on the pirate ship Jerry said, "Who are you? What do you want?"

"We want your fire rockets and space guns," said the man. "As to who we are, let's say we are friends of a friend of yours."

"A friend of a friend of ours?" asked Jerry. "Who...?"

All at once Matt's voice came over the open spacetalker. "Jerry, don't give in to them. This ship is roll..." Then Matt's voice was cut off.

"You see," said the voice again. "We are not small after all. We do have guns to back us up. Now, about those fire rockets....."

All at once Jerry and Scotty heard the man in the engine room call out. "No good pirates! With one shot I can cut your ship in two!" And with that the man opened up on the pirate ship with his space shotgun.

"No, don't fire!" Scotty called out. "Matt is on that ship!"

But it was no use. The guns were roaring. And with the sounds of those guns, the man did not hear Scotty's call to hold the fire.

Now the pirate ship opened up. Its first shots were close, but they did not hit the *SS-14*. Scotty heard Jerry open fire with his space shotgun. He knew that it would not be long before the pirate ship gunned them down.

"Right you are," came back the pirate's voice. "And you can have him back—for your rockets and space guns. But if you don't give us what we want—well, take a look at our spaceship."

Jerry and Scotty could see the pirate ship with their own eyes. It had moved in very close, along the left side of the *SS-14*.

The spaceship was headed right for them. As the two men watched, the sides of the pirate ship opened. Through the openings came the ends of space guns. They were big guns and the pirate ship had more space guns than the *SS-14*.

Scotty rolled the *SS-14* to the right, bringing the two ships head-on. "Now if I can get the *Point Speed* between us and the pirate ship," Scotty said to himself, "the wreck will take the hits from the pirate's guns."

But the load of *Point Speed* was too much for *SS-14*. It could not get the *SS-14* around. All at once a load of spaceshot hit one of the rocket engines on the spacesweeper. *SS-14* turned on its side and rolled back to the left, right in front of the pirate ship. Then another load of spaceshot hit the *SS-14*.

All at once Scotty thought he saw another pirate ship firing on them. It was behind the first pirate ship and closing in fast. Then lights were going on and off in front of Scotty's eyes. The lights were coming closer and closer, getting bigger and bigger. Scotty had the feeling—the funny feeling—that his air had been cut off. His eyes rolled back in his head. Then the lights went out!

❖❖❖❖❖❖❖❖

Scotty could feel the air. It was hitting his right eye and running up over his head. Air was what he wanted. He knew that. As he turned his head more to the right, Scotty knew where the air was coming from. And he knew why he wanted it. There was a hole in the top of his space suit!

Slowly, all of the air was going out of his suit. It would not be long before it would all be gone. There was still a little air running through the front of the spaceship, but not much. Scotty had to have more.

Scotty placed his hand over the hole in the suit. He could feel the air coming out through the hole. Scotty's hand closed over a small can of suit-sealer he had placed under his seat. He took sealer out of the can and placed it over the hole. The air stopped coming out.

"What happened?" Scotty asked himself. "There was a light, then....I thought I saw a rocketship...." Then it all came back to him. "A rocketship!"

Scotty looked out into space. There was no ship there. The pirates were gone. Scotty looked around the inside of the *SS-14*. All but one of the lights went out.

Scotty could just see Jerry. His friend was still bolted into his seat, but he was not moving. Scotty looked for holes in the top and sides of *SS-14*. He could not see any. He turned to the airmaker. It had stopped running. He hit it with his hand and the airmaker came on. He could feel the air on his face. "One good thing," thought Scotty, "We still have air."

Scotty got out of his seat and moved to Jerry's side. The ship seemed to be on its side and Scotty had to move slowly. He took out a small handlight he had in his belt. He turned the light on Jerry's face. Scotty could see a cut over Jerry's right eye. But his friend was getting air and using it.

Just then Scotty heard something behind him. He pulled out his small handgun and turned. The light cut through the dark room. Standing just inside the door were two men. Scotty was about to fire when—

"Don't fire that gun, Scotty!" said one of the men. "We are Space Police!"

Scotty took a long, close look. Then he saw the gray space suits the men had on. The men were Space Police.

Scotty was more than glad to see them. The Space Police could be of help to him right now.

"Give me a hand with Jerry," said Scotty to the man closest to him. To the other man he said, "See if you can get some lights in here. And see how the man is in the engine room."

By now Jerry was coming around. He saw Scotty standing over him. "What is going on?" he asked.

"You got hit on the head," said Scotty.

Just then the lights came on all over the spaceship. Scotty looked around at the spacefeeler board. It was a wreck. All of its lights were out. There were holes in the board. Scotty turned to the man standing at his side. "You got here just in time," he said. "It would not have been long before that pirate shot us down." Then he asked, "How did you find us?"

"We just happened by," said the man. "We saw that ship firing on you and we came running."

Scotty said, "Just before I blacked out, I thought I saw another ship firing. It was you. Now I know I was not seeing things."

"But Matt? Where is Matt?" asked Jerry, holding his head in his hands.

"Who is Matt?" the man asked.

"Matt Miles," said Scotty to the man. "You know him. He is in the Space Police. And he is on that pirate ship!"

"The pirate ship got away," the man said to Jerry. "It was too fast for us. If Miles was on it, well..."

"Then let's get these wrecks back to Earth," said Jerry, standing up. "We have a lot of work to do if we are going to get Miles back from Roll See."

"Roll See?" said Scotty. "How do you know it was Roll See?"

"I know it now," said Jerry. "He..."

"One of the men cut in and asked, "Roll See, the pirate? That can't be. Roll See is..."

"Dead?" said Jerry. "That's what you think. He is out there in a spaceship. And he has Matt. We are going after them. Now, let's get rolling."

(1628)

Roll See, the Pirate

Jerry was right about who ran the pirate ship. It was Roll See. After getting away from the Space Police, Roll See had headed the big pirate spaceship out into space.

Roll See walked through his ship. It was a good spaceship. It was no big spaceworker's ship and it did not have the room that a spacesweeper had. But the pirate ship could do things that other spaceships could not do.

The pirate ship could get off fire rockets from both ends of the ship. She could fire loads of spaceshot from places above her rocket engines. And the pirate ship was fast, very fast! The only spaceships that could go faster were the Space Police *Speed Rockets*. And Roll See had not seen one of them for years. They used too much gas.

Roll See opened the door to a small room in the top of the ship. Seated in the room, with his back to Roll See, was Matt Miles.

Roll See had not seen Matt when the man came on board. He knew that this man had called out over the open spacetalker in the room to the men on the space-sweeper. But they had cut him off. Roll See liked Matt for that. "He would make a good pirate," Roll See thought.

"Good day, Miles," said the pirate. "Do you find our little ship to your liking?"

Matt turned around. He took one look at Roll See's face, then looked away. "Your face, man!" said Matt. "What happened to it?"

Roll See ran his hand over his face. "It is the fire on our planet," he said. "When my men were in their space suits, you did not see their faces. They all look like this. Our faces and hands have been made this dark by the roaring fires of that—that place! We have been on the Fire Planet for years and years. You do not know what it is like to live on a planet of fire, do you?"

"The Fire Planet!" said Matt. "Then you must be the pirate Roll See, just as Jerry and Scotty thought."

"I'm Roll See all right," said the man. "The top space pirate of them all. The shipwrecker. I have been dead 15 years now. Or so they have thought. Could I be dead, standing here before you? You say my face looks like it. What do you think?"

"But no man comes back from the Fire Planet," said Matt. "How could it be? You went down and..."

"But we did come back," said Roll See. "After 15 years, we came back. To this day I can see the Space Police ship that ran us down. Our ship was out of gas. We came down on the far side of the planet—in an open place where there was air."

"Air?" asked Matt. "On the Fire Planet?"

"There is air," said Roll See. "But there is fire, too. You can feel it all the time—on your hands, on your face. It is all around you, but not in this open place."

Roll See stopped, then he went on. "Two of our engines were wrecked. We could not get off the planet. But we had canned goods and water."

"We were on the planet a long time," said Roll See. "Years, it was. Then, just as our water and canned goods were giving out, another ship came down. The men in it were dead before the ship hit. But the ship was loaded with water and canned goods. Later a big pirate ship was wrecked close to us. These men were dead, too. But two of the ship's engines were still working. We put them on our spaceship and took off."

"So your pirate ship is the one that has been seen over Tookk and Way?" said Matt. "And you shot down the *Point Speed*."

"Right again," said Roll See. "Now and then we make a sweep into space, picking up what we have to have. When we took on the *Point Speed*, we had to have her fire rockets and spaceshot. The men on *Point Speed* did not know what hit them. We came up behind her and..."

"Don't go on," said Matt. "I saw what you did. Where are you taking me?"

"Back to the Fire Planet," said Roll See. "We don't like the planet—in a way—for what it did to us. But in another way we do like it. No spaceships come close to it. The Space Police don't know there is air on the planet. They don't know we are there."

"Why did you come back to *Point Speed*?" Matt asked.

"To get that paper," said Roll See. "I should not have left it there in the first place. When we wrecked the *Point Speed*, I thought I would let the Space Police know that Roll See was back. It was the first Space Police rocket we had hit. After I did it, though, I knew the Space Police would come looking for me. We came back to get the paper, and the ship was gone. We picked you up on our spacefeeler board as the *SS-14* let go of you over Planet Way."

"One more thing," said Matt. "Why did you go back to the wreck again—when the spacesweeper was there?"

"I thought the men on the spacesweeper must have the paper," said Roll See. "And I wanted their spaceshot and fire rockets. I did not know they had gone back to Earth. I wanted that paper back. And you know, dead men do not tell what they know."

"But my friends in the Space Police know who you are now," said Matt. "They will find us. You will see."

The pirate laughed. "I have thought of that," he said. "That is why you are not dead now. They will not do a thing to us, not with you on board. But they can't catch us. They can't find us. Good day, Matt Miles." With that the pirate left, closing the door behind him.

Matt ran to the door, but he could not pull it open. He went back to his seat and closed his eyes. But Matt could not get away from the picture of Roll See's face.

(1052)

Stand By to Board

Once they were back on Earth, Jerry and Scotty went to see the head man of the Space Police. Jerry told the man what had happened: that Roll See now had Matt on board his pirate spaceship.

"You just think it was Roll See," said the man.

"It was Roll See, all right," said Jerry. "I heard Matt say so over the open spacetalker."

"But how do you know that, Jerry?" Scotty asked. "All I heard was Matt saying something about the ship rolling before he was cut off."

"He did not say the ship was rolling," Jerry said. "He was going to say 'the ship is Roll See's'! But he was cut off."

"Say, that could have been it!" said Scotty. "But if it is Roll See, where is he taking Matt?"

"To the Fire Planet!" said Jerry.

"What are you talking about?" said Scotty. "There can be no men on the Fire Planet."

"Those pirates have to be coming and going from there," said Jerry. "There is no other planet they could work from. There are men on all of the other planets around there. I don't know how Roll See brings it off, but he and his pirates work off the Fire Planet."

Jerry asked, "Will the Space Police give us a *Speed Rocket* and twenty men? It could be a long shot, but I think we can head off Roll See's pirate ship with one of our fast *Speed Rockets*."

"You will have the ship and the men in an hour," said the man.

"Come on, Scotty!" said Jerry. "We have work to do."

51

With a great roar the *Speed Rocket* took off. Jerry, Scotty and the twenty men were in it. The Space Police *Speed Rockets* were very fast. There were no faster ships in space. These ships were not used very much. With their great speed they could not be turned and stopped in space as could spacesweepers like the *SS-14*. They used too much gas, too. But in a speed run, there was no faster ship. And speed was what Jerry and Scotty had to have if they were to catch Roll See's pirate ship.

For two days the *Speed Rocket* roared on into space.
Faster and faster it seemed to go. One time the men
picked up something on the spacefeeler board. "Move the
ship one point to the right, Scotty," said Jerry.

Scotty moved the ship and looked out to see a meteor
as they went by it. "Jerry, did you see that?" asked Scotty.
"It was a meteor. It is going the way we are going. And
we went right by it. The meteor looked as if it was standing still!"

"I know it," said Jerry. "The *Speed Rocket* is fast!"

On and on into space went the *Speed Rocket*. One after
another the planets were left behind: Tookk and Way, the
Dead Planet, and the Planet Eye. Then, just as the *Speed
Rocket* came out of a meteor belt—

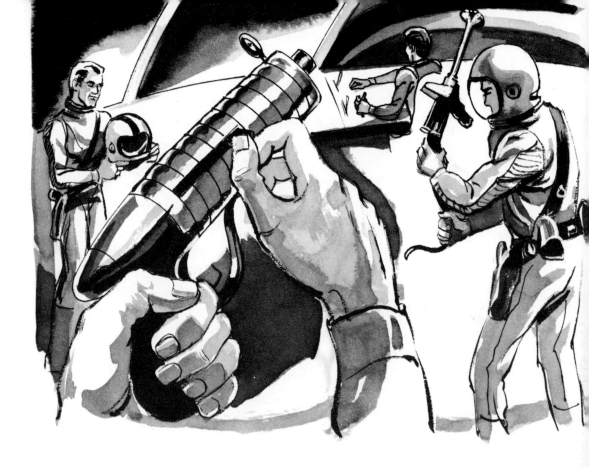

Jerry turned on the ship's inside-talker. "Now hear this, men," he said. "We think we have picked up the pirate ship. It is still 20,000 miles away. When we catch up to the ship, all of us will have our work cut out for us. Scotty is coming back there with you to pick out two men who will stand by with sealer to close up holes in this ship if it gets hit with spaceshot. One other man is to be picked to stand by the spacefeeler board to take the place of Scotty and me when we go on board the pirate ship."

"And we want 10 men to board the pirate ship with us," said Scotty. "These men are to have on space suits. They are to have their gas guns in their belts. They will be using them. All of the other men are to man the fire rockets and the space shotguns. That is all."

Jerry sent Scotty back to talk to the men. Then he turned back to the spacefeeler board. He did not take his eyes off it as they moved closer and closer to the ship ahead. The *Speed Rocket* had been roaring along at top speed. Now Jerry slowed the ship so that it would not go by the pirate ship in front of them.

Jerry knew that the men in the pirate ship had not seen them. The Pirate ship did not move to its right or left. It did not speed up or slow down. Jerry pulled the *Speed Rocket* right up to the pirate ship. He wanted to see it up close with his own eyes. Then he would know—

He knew! There were the openings for the space shotguns. There were the openings for the fire rockets. It was the ship that had fired on them. It was Roll See, the pirate!

As Scotty came through the door, Jerry said into the inside-talker, "All hands! We have found the pirate ship. It is where we thought it would be. Look to your gas guns, men. That is all."

"Close up on the pirate ship, Scotty," said Jerry. Then he turned on the open spacetalker, and sent out a call.

"Space Police *Speed Rocket* calling pirate ship *Roll See!* Space Police *Speed Rocket* calling pirate ship *Roll See.* Do you hear me? Over!"

"They heard you, Jerry," said Scotty. "Look at those side guns they are bringing around and pointing our way."

"It will do them no good," said Jerry. "This *Speed Rocket* is so fast it can run away from their guns."

"I hope you are right about that," said Scotty.

There was a funny sound over the open spacetalker, then a voice. "Calling Space Police *Speed Rocket*. We are not a pirate ship. But what do you want?"

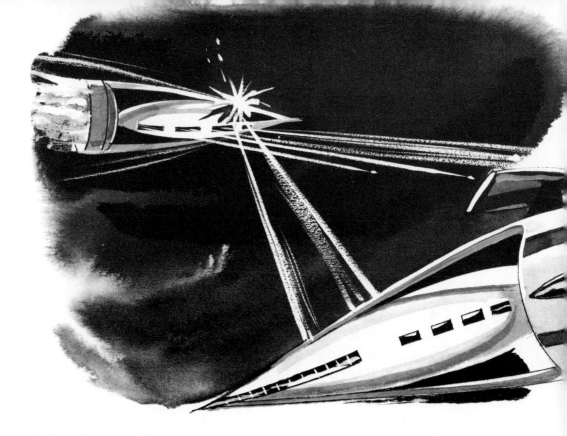

"We want you to pull up and stop, Roll See," said Jerry. "We know it is you."

The open spacetalker was still, then a voice came back. "All right, this is Roll See, the pirate. You will not stop us, though. Turn that ship around and get out of here before we fire on you!"

"Pull up, pirate ship!" said Jerry. To Scotty, he said, "Bring the ship around to the right, Scotty! Fast!"

Jerry knew what he was doing. For just as Scotty pulled the ship around, spaceshot roared from the guns of the pirate ship. If the rocketship had not moved...

Then Jerry called to his men. "Stand by all hands! We are going in! Under him, Scotty. Get in under him. There are no guns there. Magnets on! Those of you who are going on board—space suits on! Guns out!"

Scotty took the *Speed Rocket* in.. fast....then under... and up. He heard the two ships hit. Then there was a man at his side to take over for him. Scotty ran to the back of the ship. Jerry was ahead of him. The 10 men that Scotty had picked were there with their space suits on.

"Cut through into the pirate ship," Jerry said to one of his men. "Let's get in there."

Working fast, the man cut a hole into the pirate ship. Guns up, Jerry, Scotty and their men ran through the opening. The men found they were in a small room with fire rockets in it. The rocket keep! But there were no pirates.

The door to the rocket keep was closed. Jerry knew that the other rooms in the pirate ship would hold their air. But if the door was opened—

One man moved to open the door. "Don't do that!" Scotty told the man. "Matt is in there. And if you open that door, all the air in there will run out."

"Seal the opening we came through," said Jerry. "Get a move on."

The opening in the ship was closed. Then the men moved to the closed door. Jerry could hear men on the other side of the door. The men were running.

"Now, men!" Jerry called out.

With that he pulled open the door and went through it, his gun roaring! (1363)

With Boarding Picks

Before him were many men. The faces were those of men who had been in a fire: cut, open, and black. One man was putting up a big gas gun. Jerry downed the man with one shot from his own gas gun. Another two men went down under his fire. Behind him, the men from the Space Police came through the door. Their guns roared right and left.

Then there were men all over the room. Sounds and voices were heard as men called out; guns went off; right fists to the head came after left fists to the face; men went down, got up, only to go down again. Then the men from the Space Police were standing over the pirates.

"Good work, men", said Scotty. "Pick up that big gas gun. There are more pirates than this. We can use the gun against them. And keep an eye out for Matt!"

One of the men turned the gun on a door. Fire shot out of the end of the gun. It cut right through the door and into a side room.

"All right, now," said Scotty. "Let's keep together and keep moving. We will work from the back end of the ship to the front. I will go first with the gas gun."

"You there," said Jerry to a big man. "Bring the stand for Scotty's gun."

Scotty turned the gun on another door. Down it went.

The Space Police went through it, and ran head-on into more of Roll See's men! The men were in a small room. Scotty put down the gun and used his fists, too. So did the other Space Police. Some of the Space Police went down. So did Roll See's men.

A pirate hit Jerry over the head with his gun. Jerry went down. The man was about to hit Jerry again when Scotty cut down the man with his hand gun. "Good going, friend," Jerry called out as he went after another space pirate.

It was not long before it was all over. All of Roll See's men in the room were down. Two men from the Space Police had cuts on their heads. "Now to the top of the ship, men!" said Scotty.

There was a roar from the men as they followed Scotty and Jerry. Through the ship they went, from room to room. They cut their way through doors with the gas gun. They cut their way through pirates with their fists.

The men came to a sealed room in the top of the ship. Jerry called out, "Open up!"

"Come in and get us!" came back a voice.

"Give me the big gun," Jerry said.

Jerry put the front end of the gun right against the door and fired. The door turned black, then was gone. Through the door Jerry saw more pirates. He fired the gun again, and two more went down.

Guns roaring, the men of the *Speed Rocket* went through the opening. Scotty moved in on a big pirate. The man pointed his gun at Scotty and fired. The gun did not go off. Then Scotty was on top of the man, and took him down. The two rolled over and over.

But a funny thing happened. A dark-faced pirate in a space suit just watched. He did not take out his gun. Jerry walked up to the pirate. "You are," said Jerry, "Roll See, head of all the space pirates."

"The pirate of the Fire Planet," said Roll See.

"Will you take me to Matt Miles?" asked Jerry.

"Right this way," said the pirate.

Jerry followed the pirate. "It is funny," Jerry thought to himself. "This man is like a pirate of days gone by. He lets his men man the guns. He uses his men. But he would not help them."

Roll See took Jerry to the very top of the spaceship.

"Jerry!" Matt said as the two men walked into a room. "Has he got your ship, too?"

Roll See laughed. "No, my friend, it is just the other way around. His men are on my ship. But it is not over. Jerry—as you call him—must face me."

"So you are going to be a pirate to the end?" said Jerry. "Just the two of us, together, having it out?"

"That is right," said the pirate.

"So be it," said Jerry. "I think, then, that I have the right to say how we will go at it."

"As you say 'so be it'," Roll See said. "And that will be...?"

"With boarding picks," said Jerry.

"Very well," said the pirate. "We have some here in the room." He walked to the other side of the room, then came back with two boarding picks. These were long black things, with points on the ends. They were used to pull spaceships together. Jerry took his pick and looked it over.

"Is your pick a good one?" asked Roll See.

"It will do," said Jerry, looking over his pick. "Tell me when you...."

"Now!" said the pirate.

In the end Jerry knew it would be this way. He was still looking at his pick when Roll See hit him. Just in time Jerry saw it coming and got his head out of the way. But the pick came down on his back.

Jerry went down. Roll See was on top of him. Jerry saw the pick coming at his head again. He rolled to the right and heard the pick go by. Jerry got up fast, with his own pick still in his hands.

Roll See was laughing now. He came at Jerry again, the end of his pick pointed right at him. Jerry got out of the way and moved around to the left.

Then the two men were in close to one another: cutting, rolling, looking for an opening. Roll See knew how to use his pick. He did not give up. In and out went the two men, then up and back through the room, belting away with their picks.

Jerry worked Roll See to one side of the room. All at once Jerry made a move with his pick as if to hit the pirate in the head. Roll See's pick came up. Jerry came up under Roll See's pick with his own. All of the feeling went out of the pirate's hands. He could not hold the pick. The pirate let go of it. Bringing his pick up again, Jerry hit the pirate on the top of the head. Down he went and was still. It was all over.

Scotty came running into the room. He had his handgun out. Then he saw Roll See, with Matt and Jerry standing over him.

"Matt! Jerry" Scotty said. "Are you all right?"

"It's all over, Scotty," said Jerry. "How did it go with you?"

"We have things well in hand," said Scotty. "Tell me, what happened to Roll See?"

Matt looked at Scotty and said, "Jerry *picked* on him."

"But I hit him in the right place," said Jerry. "He was the *head* pirate."

Scotty looked at his two friends. "So you two think you are funny!" he said. "Come on, men, let's get down to Earth." He threw the boarding pick against a wall.

They all laughed and walked out of the room. (1129)

(10,098)

Space

There is no limit to space. It continues in all directions. Such an idea is almost beyond man's power of thought. Many people use the word *galaxy* to give space some boundary. A galaxy is made up of billions of stars, all whirling through space. Our sun is one of the stars in a galaxy. The planet earth and other planets circle in space around the sun. The moon moves through space around the earth. Telescopes can see other galaxies beyond the one our earth is in.

Where does space begin? We usually say space begins about 100 miles above the earth. At that height, the earth's air is very thin. An object moving through the air 100 miles above earth will not be slowed very much. But near or on the earth's surface, that same object would not move as fast because the air is heavier.

Think about the following statements. Be prepared to explain.

1. Space has no beginning and no end.

2. The moon is in a galaxy with earth.

3. Space begins 100 miles above the earth.

4. Air is lighter on the surface of the earth than on the moon.

Spaceman

Walter Marty Schirra, Jr. was born in Hackensack, New Jersey on March 12, 1923. As a boy, Walter Schirra learned to fly. His early interest in flying came from his father, a World War I pilot, and from his mother, a stunt flier.

In October of 1962, Walter Schirra made six flights around the earth in a spacecraft named Sigma 7. In December of 1965, Schirra was the pilot of Gemini 6, a spaceship which accomplished man's first rendezvous or meeting in space. With the help of astronaut Thomas Stafford, Schirra guided his spacecraft close to Gemini 7, a spaceship piloted by Frank Borman and James Lovell. The two spaceships locked together when they were 185 miles above the Pacific Ocean. It was not a simple job. Schirra's Gemini 6 chased Gemini 7 for more than 100,000 miles at speeds of 17,500 miles per hour before the two craft docked together as one.

1. How old was Walter Schirra when he became interested in flying?

2. Where did Schirra get his interest in flying?

3. What were the names of the spacecraft in which Walter Schirra flew?

4. What was Walter Schirra's greatest space achievement?

Spacecraft

The most famous launch vehicles are part of a project named Apollo 11. Using a big launch spacecraft called Saturn V, the United States landed astronauts Neil Armstrong and Edwin Aldrin, Jr. on the moon on July 20, 1969. Before taking off, this giant vehicle stood 360 feet tall and weighed 260,000 pounds.

Saturn V was not alone at take off. Riding on its nose were Columbia and Eagle, two smaller spacecraft. Once these two linked space vehicles went into orbit around the moon, Armstrong and Aldrin left the Columbia, climbed into Eagle, and flew down to the moon. Astronaut Michael Collins stayed in Columbia while his two friends explored the moon. Later, Eagle took off from the moon, met with Columbia in space and the astronauts returned safely to earth.

Think about the following statements. Which word or words in the article would complete each sentence?

1. Neil Armstrong and Edwin Aldrin landed on the moon in a small spacecraft named....

2. At launching time, Saturn V weighed....

3. Michael Collins was pilot of a spacecraft known as....

Space Deed

The conquest of space began hundreds of years ago. When speaking of the early history of space flight, one must think of almost unknown scientists who, little by little, added bits and pieces to man's knowledge of space and space travel.

Over 400 years ago a scientist named Johannes Kepler described clearly the way heavenly bodies, like moons and planets, move in space. The laws he laid down then help to plan the flights of spaceships today.

In 1687, Sir Isaac Newton published a book entitled *Laws of Motion.* Sir Isaac's laws had to do with motion. His third law stated that for every action there is an opposite and equal reaction. This law describes why a rocket takes off. The engine of the rocket shoots exhaust backward into space. The reaction to the exhaust drives the rocket forward or upward.

Robert Goddard and Hermann Oberth are sometimes called "the fathers of space flight." Goddard's interests in 1919 were in liquid fuel rockets and flight to the moon. Oberth wrote a book in 1923 describing a possible spaceship.

Think about the following statements. Be prepared to explain your answers. Which deeds or actions do you think about when you read the names?

1. Robert Goddard

2. Johannes Kepler

3. Sir Isaac Newton

4. Hermann Oberth

Vocabulary

The total vocabulary of this book is 272 words, excluding proper names and sound words. The 28 words in roman type should be familiar to children reading on a second-grade level. The 20 words above second-grade level are shown in italic type. The number indicates the page on which the word first appears.

against 12
answered 14

belt 7
between 7
board 5
bolted 41

darkness 12
dead 5

Earth 6
engines 5
feel 6
fifteen 21
forgot 30

gas 16
gun 14

happened 14
hour 51

listen 8
load 14
lot 14

magnets 14
meteors 6
miles 5

outside 15
piece 36

pirates 9
planets 9
pointing 56

quite 30

rocket 6

sealed 22
seat 6
seemed 41

ship 5
shot 6
sound 10
space 5
speed 6
sped 13
suits 15
sweep 6

taken 15
those 5
though 57
toward 12
twenty 51

wreck 5
writing 21

The number in parentheses on the last page of each chapter indicates the total number of words in that chapter. The number underlined on the last page of the story indicates the total number of words in the entire story.

72   Editor
                           Ruth Lommatzsch